My dearest puppy, Storm,

I hope this letter reaches you safe and sound. You have been so brave since you had to flee from the evil wolf Shadow.

Do not worry about me. I will hide here until you are strong enough to return and lead our pack. For now you must move on – you must hide from Shadow and his spies. If Shadow finds this letter I believe he will try to destroy it . . .

Find a good friend – someone to help finish my message to you. Because what I have to say to you is important. What I have to say is this: you must always

Please don't feel lonely. Trust in your friends and all will be well.

Your loving mother,

Canista

Sue Bentley's books for children often include animals, fairies and wildlife. She lives in Northampton and enjoys reading, going to the cinema, relaxing by her garden pond and watching the birds feeding their babies on the lawn. At school she was always getting told off for daydreaming or staring out of the window – but she now realizes that she was storing up ideas for when she became a writer. She has met and owned many cats and dogs and each one has brought a special kind of magic to her life.

Sue Bentley

Magic Puppy

Muddy Paws

Illustrated by Angela Swan

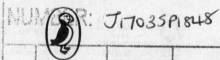

To Petra — a gentle sheepdog friend

and a loyal companion

PUFFIN BOOKS

Published by the Penguin Group
Penguin Books Ltd, 80 Strand, London WC2R ORL, England
Penguin Group (USA) Inc., 375 Hudson Street, New York, New York 10014, USA
Penguin Group (Canada), 90 Eglinton Avenue East, Suite 700, Toronto, Ontario, Canada M4P 2Y3
(a division of Pearson Penguin Canada Inc.)
Penguin Ireland, 25 St Stephen's Green, Dublin 2, Ireland (a division of Penguin Books Ltd)
Penguin Group (Australia), 250 Camberwell Road, Camberwell, Victoria 3124, Australia
(a division of Pearson Australia Group Pty Ltd)
Penguin Books India Pvt Ltd, 11 Community Centre, Panchsheel Park, New Delhi – 110 017, India
Penguin Group (NZ), 67 Apollo Drive, Rosedale, North Shore 0632, New Zealand
(a division of Pearson New Zealand Ltd)
Penguin Books (South Africa) (Pty) Ltd, 24 Sturdee Avenue, Rosebank,
Johannesburg 2196, South Africa

Penguin Books Ltd, Registered Offices: 80 Strand, London WC2R ORL, England

puffinbooks.com

First published 2008
020

Text copyright © Sue Bentley, 2008
Illustrations copyright © Angela Swan, 2008
All rights reserved

The moral right of the author and illustrator has been asserted

Set in Bembo
Typeset by Palimpsest Book Production Limited, Grangemouth, Stirlingshire
Made and printed in England by Clays Ltd, St Ives plc

British Library Cataloguing in Publication Data
A CIP catalogue record for this book is available from the British Library

ISBN: 978-0-141-32351-0

www.greenpenguin.co.uk

Prologue

Storm paused to lap up thirstily the clear water that flowed swiftly between two banks of ice. It felt good to be back in his home world.

But the young silver-grey wolf's happiness lasted for only a moment as he thought of his mother, Canista, wounded and in hiding.

Suddenly a terrifying howl echoed on the icy wind.

'Shadow!' Storm gasped, realizing that the fierce lone wolf was close.

There was a bright flash and a dazzling shower of golden sparks. Where Storm had been standing there now crouched a tiny fluffy black-and-white Border collie puppy with midnight-blue eyes.

Storm trembled, hoping that his puppy disguise would protect him from the evil Shadow. Keeping his little belly low to the ground, Storm crept into a clump of snow-covered bushes.

A dark shape pushed through the bushes, loosening a cloud of snow, and Storm's tiny heart missed a beat. Shadow had found him!

But instead of the lone wolf's dark-grey muzzle and pitiless black eyes, Storm saw a familiar silver-grey face with bright golden eyes.

'Mother!' he yapped with relief.

'I am glad you are safe and well, my son, but you have returned at a dangerous time,' Canista said in a warm velvety growl. She nuzzled the disguised cub's black-and-white face, but then gave a sharp wince of pain.

'Shadow's poisonous bite sapped your strength!' Storm blew out a gentle stream of tiny gold sparks, which sank into Canista's injured leg and disappeared.

'Thank you, Storm. The pain is easing. But there isn't time right now for you to help me recover all my

3

powers. You must go – Shadow is very close,' Canista rumbled softly.

Sadness rippled through Storm's tiny puppy body as he thought of his dead father and litter brothers and the once proud Moon-claw wolf pack, now broken up. His midnight-blue eyes flashed with anger. 'One day I will stand beside you and face Shadow!'

Canista nodded proudly. 'But until then, you must hide in the other world. Use this disguise and return when your magic is stronger.'

Another fierce howl split the air. 'I know you are close! Come out and let us finish this!' Shadow cried in an icy growl.

'Go now, Storm! Save yourself!' Canista urged.

Bright gold sparks ignited in the tiny black-and-white puppy's fur. Storm whined softly as he felt the power building inside him. Golden light pooled brightly around him. And grew brighter . . .

Chapter
ONE

Beth Hollis woke with a start and lay looking up at the unfamiliar white ceiling with its low black beams. Rain pattered against the window and she could hear birdsong, animal noises and voices outside.

Gradually Beth recognized the attic bedroom in Tail End Farm owned by her aunt and uncle. She was staying here while her parents were away.

The room was still quite dark and a gust of wind sent more rain drumming against the window. Beth pulled the duvet over her head and snuggled back under the downy warmth.

Suddenly the bedroom door banged open. Beth heard muffled footsteps approaching the bed and then she felt a

rush of cool air as the duvet was twitched aside.

'Rise and shine!' cried a cheeky voice. 'Mornings start early on a farm!'

'Hey!' Beth complained, sitting bolt upright.

Martin Badby, her tall dark-haired cousin, stood grinning mischievously down at her.

'Give that back!' Beth demanded, lungeing at him with outstretched arms.

'No chance!' Martin crowed, backing away. He tossed the duvet across the room out of her reach.

Beth scowled. Martin was twelve years old, older than her by three years, but he sometimes acted as if he was aged about six. He loved playing silly jokes on people, especially his younger cousin.

'That was a really mean thing to do!' she fumed.

'Yeah? So sue me!' Martin said cheerfully. 'Are you coming downstairs, then?'

Beth sat in the middle of her bed and crossed her arms. 'No, I am not! Auntie Em said I needn't get up early on my first day here!'

'That's only cos you were sulking last night. I heard you talking to your mum and dad before they left. "Poor me. It's *so* awful having to stay at boring old Tail End,"' he mimicked in a silly whiny little voice.

'I don't talk like that!' Beth said, feeling her cheeks redden. 'Anyway, how would you like it if you got dumped on relatives while your parents flew off to America for two weeks?'

Martin rolled his eyes. 'They're not exactly going to Disney World, are they? It's only some boring old business trip.'

'I still wanted to go with them,' Beth murmured. She'd never been apart from her parents, except for the occasional night's sleepover at a friend's house and she was really going to miss them.

'Talk about selfish. I don't s'pose you even thought about me?' Martin grumbled.

Beth frowned, puzzled. 'What about you?'

'Well, *I've* got to put up with *you*, haven't I? Mum and Dad have

practically ordered me to look after you.
Just what I wanted, my dopey spoiled
cousin trailing round after me – not!'

'Thanks very much! I'll try not to get
in your way!' Beth cried indignantly.
She flung herself off the bed and
stomped over to the wardrobe. 'Can you
go out now, please? I want to get
dressed.'

'Thought you weren't getting up?'
Martin crowed.

'I've changed my mind. Spoiled
cousins do that a lot, you know!' Beth
said spiritedly.

'Whatever!' Martin went out and
closed the bedroom door behind him.

Beth pulled a face at the closed door.
She'd forgotten just how annoying her
cousin could be and now it seemed that

he wasn't keen on having her here at all. Her spirits sank even further as she thought of the two weeks stretching endlessly ahead of her.

'Morning, Beth. You're up early. Did you sleep well?' Emily Badby called from the yard as Beth stood in the open doorway of the back porch.

'Fine, thanks,' Beth replied. *No thanks to Martin*, she thought.

Her aunt held a bucket of vegetable trimmings. 'Goats love a nibble of fresh food. It gets them in a good mood for milking. Do you want to come and watch?'

'OK,' Beth said, shrugging. She wasn't that interested in goats, but there was still ages before breakfast and nothing much else to do.

She borrowed a spare mac and some wellies and followed her aunt into the barn. A sweetish musty smell of goats, dung and warm hay greeted her. 'Phew!' Beth wrinkled her nose.

Emily Badby laughed. 'It's a healthy farm smell. You'll get used to it.'

Beth wasn't sure she wanted to. She

went to look at the brown-and-white
goats in their neat pens, ranged down
one side of the barn. 'They all look a
bit fed up. What sort are they?' she
asked.

'Anglo-Nubians. It's their long noses
and lop ears that give them that
expression,' Emily explained, selecting a
goat and leading it to a small wooden
platform. The goat leapt up nimbly and
soon Beth was watching the creamy
milk foaming into a spotlessly clean
bucket. 'I sell milk, yogurt and cheese in
the local shops,' Emily said. 'My dairy's
next door. You can have a look round
sometime, but ask me first. I have strict
rules about hygiene.'

Beth nodded.

Her aunt soon finished milking. She

then poured the milk through a filter into a metal churn. 'I'll just take this to the dairy and then get started on breakfast.'

A loud braying noise came from the back of the barn. 'Oh! What's that?' Beth looked round in surprise.

Her aunt laughed. 'That's Darcy, my new billy goat. He's only been here for a week or so, but he's always complaining because he isn't getting any attention.'

'Can I go and say hello to him?' Beth asked.

'Yes, of course, but be –' The rest of her aunt's reply was drowned out by a loud irritable voice in the doorway.

'There you are!' Martin cried,

standing aside as his mum went out. 'What are you hiding in here for?'

'I wasn't hiding! Auntie Em said I could watch her milking,' Beth said.

Martin flicked back a lock of wet dark hair. 'Anyway, Dad said I had to ask you if you wanted to come with me to take Ella for a walk.' Ella was the family's old black-and-white Welsh Border collie.

'No thanks,' Beth said, feeling miffed that he'd only asked her because his dad had made him. Turning on her heel, she went towards the back of the barn. 'I'm going to look at Darcy.'

'Hang on! I'll come with you. Ella won't mind waiting for her walk. I have to drag her out half the time anyway. Since Dad retired her from

farm work, she's really stiffened up,'
Martin said.

Darcy's pen was behind some straw
bales. He was a handsome dark-brown
goat with a white neck. 'It looks as if
he's wearing a smart white collar!' Beth
exclaimed as Darcy lifted his head and
gave an inquisitive snicker.

Martin undid the latch and gestured

for Beth to go into the pen ahead of him.

Beth hesitated. 'Are you sure it's safe to go in?'

'Course,' Martin said. 'Are you chicken or what?'

Beth took two steps into the pen. Suddenly, she felt Martin shove her in the back and heard the gate slam shut. She shot forward and almost went sprawling in the straw.

'You idiot!' she cried, whirling round just in time to see Martin jogging away through the barn. 'That's not funny!' she shouted after him.

There was a bawl of protest from behind her. Beth turned back to see Darcy curling his lips and eyeing her suspiciously.

She swallowed. 'N-nice goat.'

Darcy lowered his head. He looked like he was going to charge!

Chapter
TWO

Beth's heart rose into her mouth.
Suddenly there was a dazzling flash of
gold light and a big shower of bright
gold sparks sprinkled all around her and
Darcy. Blinded for a moment, she
rubbed her eyes. Beth tensed as she felt
a peculiar warm, tingly feeling down
her spine.

When she could see again, she

noticed that Darcy was frozen to the
spot and standing between the goat's
legs was a tiny fluffy black-and-white
puppy with enormous midnight-blue
eyes. Specks of gold dust seemed to be
glimmering among its fur.

'What's going on?' Beth exclaimed.

The tiny puppy drew itself up. 'I am
Storm of the Moon-claw pack. I have
arrived from a place that is far from
here.'

'Y-you can talk?' Beth gasped in total amazement.

Suddenly, the penny dropped. This was obviously another of her cousin's practical jokes. She looked around, expecting Martin to jump out triumphantly.

But there was no sign of him. Beth slowly looked back to where Storm was blinking up at her, and Darcy was still standing as if he was carved from stone.

'I don't get this,' she said, puzzled.

The fluffy black-and-white puppy took a few steps towards her on big soft paws that seemed too large for his tiny body. 'I used my magic to stop this animal before it could hurt you,' Storm woofed. 'Who are you?'

'I'm B-Beth H-Hollis,' Beth
stammered.

Storm bowed his head. 'I am
honoured to meet you, Beth.'

Beth was still having trouble taking
this in. 'Um . . . me too. But . . . who
are you? *What* are you?'

Storm didn't answer. Instead, there
was another bright golden flash.

'Oh!' Beth found herself outside
Darcy's pen. Behind her the goat
snickered contentedly and she heard
him moving about in the straw,
obviously none the worse for being
temporarily put on hold.

Beth looked around for the puppy.
But it had disappeared and standing in
its place outside the pen with her there
crouched a magnificent young silver-

grey wolf with glowing midnight-blue eyes. Large gold sparks glowed in the thick ruff round his neck.

Beth gasped, eyeing the wolf's sharp teeth. 'Storm?'

'Yes, it is me, Beth. Do not be afraid,' Storm said in a deep velvety growl.

Before Beth could get used to the sight of the amazing young wolf there was a final dazzling flash of gold light

and Storm was once again a tiny fluffy black-and-white puppy.

'Wow! That's an amazing disguise. No one would ever know you're a wolf!' Beth exclaimed. 'But who are you hiding from?'

Storm began to tremble all over and his deep-blue eyes shone with anger and fear. 'Shadow is a fierce lone wolf who killed my father and all my brothers and wounded my mother with his poisoned bite. Now Shadow is looking for me. Can you help me, Beth?'

'Of course I will!' Beth's soft heart went out to him. Storm was impressive as a young wolf, but he was adorable as a tiny helpless puppy. She bent down to pick him up. 'I'll ask Auntie Em if you can stay in my room,' she said, stroking his soft little ears.

Storm leaned up to lick her chin. 'Thank you, Beth.'

'Just wait until I tell Martin about you! He's going to be so jealous!'

'No, Beth! You must tell no one my secret!' Storm said, his tiny black-and-white face very serious.

Beth didn't want to do anything that would put her new friend in danger. Besides, she reasoned, Martin had been such a pain recently that he didn't deserve to know about Storm anyway. 'OK, then,' she decided. 'It's just you and me. I promise.'

'Aren't you a bit old to be talking to an imaginary friend?' Martin said, suddenly appearing from behind the

straw bales. His eyes widened when he
saw Storm. 'Where did that cute puppy
come from?'

'I just found him. He said his name's
–' Beth stopped quickly as she realized
that she was going to have to be a lot
more careful about keeping Storm's
secret. 'I mean I'm going to call him
Storm.'

Martin's face softened for an instant.

'Ella looked just like that when she was a puppy. He must be a Border collie too. Give him to me, then.'

'I think I'll hold on to him. He's still a bit scared,' Beth said.

Martin frowned. 'Anyone would think he's yours. This is my barn, so Storm obviously belongs to me. Hand him over!' he ordered.

Beth hesitated, annoyed at being bossed about again. Martin hadn't even bothered to ask if she was OK after he'd shoved her into Darcy's pen.

'Do not worry, Beth. Do as he says,' Storm woofed.

Beth blinked in astonishment. What was Storm doing, talking to her when Martin was so close? But her cousin didn't seem to have noticed anything strange. *I hope you know what you're doing, Storm*, she thought as she reluctantly held him out towards Martin.

Smiling triumphantly, Martin went to grab Storm, but the moment he touched his black-and-white fur he jumped backwards. 'Ye-oww!' he yelled, shaking his hands in the air. 'Something just stung me! Has he got a stinging nettle in his fur or something?'

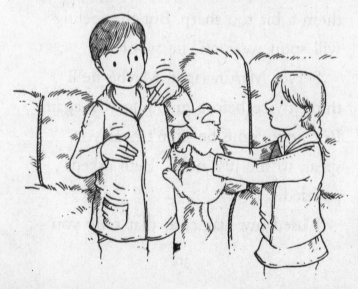

Beth pulled Storm back and held him closely again. 'I'll have a look. Maybe you should go and ask Auntie Em for some antiseptic cream.'

'Er . . . yeah,' Martin nodded as he went off, still rubbing at his hands.

'Storm!' Beth scolded gently. 'You gave him a prickle from your invisible gold sparks, didn't you?'

Storm's blue eyes twinkled mischievously. 'I think I may have made them a bit too sharp. But the feeling will soon wear off,' he woofed.

'Serves Martin right. Maybe he'll think twice before grabbing you again! But how come he didn't hear you speak to me just now?' Beth asked, puzzled.

'I used my magic, so that only you

can hear me.' Storm snuggled up in Beth's arms.

'You can do that? So I can hear you, but everyone else just hears you barking? Cool!' Beth kissed the top of his soft little head. 'Let's go and find Auntie Em. Breakfast should be almost ready. I bet you're hungry after your long journey.'

Storm's tummy rumbled and he gave an eager little bark.

As Beth went towards the farmhouse, she smiled. Her boring two weeks at Tail End Farm looked like they were going to be a lot more fun with Storm around!

Chapter
THREE

'I wonder where he came from,' Emily said thoughtfully after Beth finished telling her about Storm. 'We're quite a way from any houses out here.'

Beth looked across to where Storm was chomping a dish of dog food. Ella, the old collie, lay curled in her basket watching the puppy.

'I bet Storm was abandoned. His

owners were probably hoping some
kind person would give him a home.
Like you, Auntie Em,' Beth said
hopefully.

'I really hate people who treat animals
like that,' Martin said.

'Me too!' Beth said with feeling. It
was the first time she and Martin had
agreed on anything.

They all sat at the kitchen table,
tucking into huge farmhouse breakfasts
and big mugs of tea.

'I'm not sure it's a good time to have
a stray puppy getting under everyone's
feet,' Beth's uncle said. 'We're very busy
on the farm and no one's got time to
train him. Maybe we should take Storm
straight to the pet care centre.'

Beth's heart pounded. He couldn't

mean it! She'd only just found Storm –
she couldn't bear to lose her new friend
so quickly.

Suddenly Ella gave a rusty-sounding
bark. She got up and limped stiffly over
to Storm. The tiny puppy whined softly,
wagging his tail and wriggling his fat
little body as the old dog bent down
and gave him an experimental sniff.
Ella's eyes softened and she began
licking Storm's head.

Martin's face lit up. 'Look at that! Ella's telling us that she'll keep Storm in check. She won't let him be a pest around the farm. Way to go, old girl!'

Everyone laughed.

Beth looked at her uncle and aunt. 'So, can Storm stay? He can live in my room and I'll take him home when Mum and Dad come to fetch me,' she pleaded.

'In that case, it's fine with me. If it's OK with you, Emily,' Oliver said to his wife.

Beth's aunt gave a wry smile, but she nodded.

Beth shot over and hugged her aunt and uncle. 'Yay! Thanks a million!'

She felt so pleased that she was even ready to forgive Martin for playing mean tricks on her, but there was still one thing she wanted to tackle him about first.

Beth waited until she, Martin, Storm and Ella were walking across the fields before bringing the subject up. 'I think you should apologize for pushing me into Darcy's pen. It was a rotten thing to do,' she exclaimed.

Martin's eyes widened. 'Are you still going on about that? Can't you take a joke? Girls *always* make such a fuss.'

'Yes, because boys do such stupid things!' Beth retorted. 'I thought Darcy was going to charge at me. If it hadn't been for St– Anyway, I was lucky to get out unhurt.'

But Martin wasn't listening. He had

turned round to wait for Ella who was lagging behind. The old collie was walking stiffly with her head drooping. 'Come on, girl!' he called fondly.

At the sound of his voice, Ella tried to quicken her step, but her back legs gave way and she sat down.

'She's been doing that more and more lately,' Martin said, frowning.

Beth's anger with Martin melted away as her heart stirred with sadness at the sight of the sick old dog.

Storm glanced up at her with softly glowing eyes. 'I will fetch Ella!' he woofed gently.

Beth stood beside Martin and they watched Storm bound down the field. As soon as Storm reached the old sheepdog, he whined encouragingly and licked Ella's grey muzzle. When she just lay there panting, Storm crouched down on to his front paws and stuck his bottom in the air, inviting her to play chase.

Martin smiled at the cheeky pup's antics. 'You're wasting your time, Storm. Ella's dashing-about days are *well* over!' he called, but then his face fell and his eyes looked sad and troubled.

Beth reached out to pat his arm.

'I'm OK. Don't fuss!' Martin said, dashing a sleeve across his face.

Beth saw Storm running back and forth in front of Ella, woofing gently to encourage her until she finally heaved herself to her feet. As the old collie limped up the field, Storm ambled alongside her, keeping pace on his short legs.

'Here she comes. Good girl,' Martin crooned, stroking Ella's ears.

'Thanks, Storm,' Beth whispered to him. 'Martin might be the most annoying person in the universe, but he really loves Ella.'

The four of them walked slowly back to the farmyard in silence. As they came through the gate into the yard, Martin turned to Beth. 'Do you want to see the dairy?' he said more cheerfully.

Beth shrugged. 'I don't mind. But I thought we weren't allowed in there without permission.'

'No problem. I told Mum we might go in and she was fine about it.' Martin opened the door of a brick building, next to the barn. 'But dogs are definitely not allowed. Stay, Ella,' he ordered.

Ella sat down obediently.

'Will you wait here, please, Storm?' Beth whispered, so Martin couldn't hear. 'I won't be long.'

Storm immediately plonked down next to Ella and lay with his nose on his paws.

Martin smiled. 'Storm really catches on quickly, doesn't he? Look how he copies what Ella does. He's one bright pup!'

Beth smiled to herself. If only Martin knew how right he was!

Inside the dairy it was cool and spotlessly clean. Beth walked around, looking at the white work surfaces,

shiny metal equipment and huge
fridges, being careful not to touch
anything.

But Martin was just the opposite.
'I haven't been in here for ages. I'd
forgotten that some of this stuff's pretty
high-tech. I wonder what these do.' He
began turning some dials on a big
drum-shaped machine.

There was an ominous glugging noise.

'Should you be fiddling with that?'
Beth asked worriedly.

Martin grinned. 'You're such a
scaredy-cat. Don't panic. I'm putting the
settings back to what they were.' He
turned the dial again and the glugging
noise got louder.

Gloop. Gloop. Whoosh! Suddenly a
fountain of milk gushed out of a

narrow chute and poured on to the
floor.

'Oh heck!' Martin cried, frantically
twiddling, but the milk only sprayed
out faster.

Beth stood there in horror as a rising
tide of milk swirled round her wellies.
'Do something, Martin!'

'I'm trying to!' Martin's face was
bright red.

The door banged open and Emily
Badby swept into the dairy. Taking in
the situation with one look, she
marched over to the machine and
adjusted the dials. Seconds later, the
flow of milk slowed and then stopped.

Emily turned round with a furious
look on her face.

'Beth told me to do it!' Martin cried,
before his mum could speak.

Beth's jaw dropped. 'No, I didn't!'

Martin smirked. 'Yes, you did! Don't
try and wheedle your way out of it −'

'Be quiet! Both of you.' Emily
snapped. 'I'm very disappointed in you
both. You're not even supposed to be in
here without permission!'

Beth glared furiously at Martin. She
was really tempted to tell her aunt how

he had fibbed about having permission to come in here, but she'd never been a snitch and she wasn't about to start now.

'You know the house rules perfectly well, Martin. Besides, Beth is our guest,' Emily said stiffly, still furious. 'What have you got to say for yourself?'

Martin shrugged. 'Chill out, Mum! Don't have a major stressy! It's only a bit of old milk. It won't take long to clean up.'

'You think so?' Emily's face darkened. 'Stay there, you two! Don't you dare move!' She sloshed through the milk and opened a cupboard. 'Here!' She thrust mops and buckets at Martin and Beth. 'I want that floor spotless. Do you hear me? I'd stand and watch you, but I

have to go out now. I'll be back in an
hour, though, to check up on you. And
if you touch anything else, Martin
Badby, I'll . . . I'll have your guts for
garters!'

She swept out and a few seconds later
Beth heard a car start up and drive
away.

'Flipping heck!' Beth said, letting out
a huge sigh of relief. She'd never seen

her aunt so angry. 'I thought she was going to explode!'

'Oh, Mum's never cross for long. She'll have forgotten all about it by this evening. You don't mind cleaning up by yourself, do you? I've just remembered I've got something important to talk to Dad about,' Martin said, splashing milk everywhere as he made for the door.

'Hey! Come back –' Beth cried indignantly, but Martin had already left.

Her spirits sank as she looked down at the lake of milk. It was everywhere: under the work surfaces, sloshing round the machinery and even leaking out under the door into the yard. She hardly knew where to begin.

'Thanks for nothing, Martin,' she grumbled, angry that she'd bothered to

save him from being in even more
trouble with her aunt.

'I will help you, Beth!' Storm woofed
eagerly from the open doorway.

Beth felt a warm prickling sensation
down her spine. Something very strange
was about to happen.

Chapter
FOUR

Big gold sparks ignited in Storm's fluffy black-and-white fur and his ears and tail crackled with electricity.

Storm raised a big black front paw and a spurt of golden sparks shot out and whooshed round the dairy. They zizzed about like a swarm of busy worker bees.

Beth heard a series of faint pops as a

shimmering army of mops appeared
out of thin air and stood to attention.
As if at an invisible signal, they
began mopping the floor up and
down in neat ranks. In perfect time,
they squeezed their milky heads
into each bucket in turn. *Swish!*
Swoosh!

'This is great!' Beth said, clapping her hands with glee as the ranks of mops did their work.

In no time at all, the dairy floor was spotless. The magic mops stood to attention once more and then disappeared in a final cascade of golden sparks.

'Wow! Thanks, Storm, that was brilliant!' Beth went over and gave him a cuddle.

'You are welcome,' Storm barked happily. 'But I saw Martin going into the house. Why did he not help you?'

'That's what I want to know,' Beth said crossly. 'He made some lame excuse about talking to his dad about something. I've just about had enough of my rotten cousin. Come on, Storm, let's go and find him. I've got a few things I want to say to him!'

Storm yapped in agreement.

As Beth charged into the house with Storm towards the sitting room, she heard Uncle Ollie's voice coming through the open door and stopped in her tracks.

'It's really not fair to let Ella go on like this. She's in pain and she can hardly get about. I think it's time we called the vet in and put her to sleep,' he was saying.

'No! Please wait, Dad. Let's leave her for just a bit longer,' Martin pleaded, sounding as if he was very close to tears.

'I'm sorry, Martin. I know you love

Ella, but I'm not prepared to let
any animal suffer, however hard it
is for you to accept. We have to think
what's best for Ella. Why don't we
talk about it again tomorrow. All
right?' Oliver Badby said gently.

'OK. But I'm not changing my mind
about calling the vet and you can't
make me!' Martin said in a choked
voice.

Beth didn't wait to hear the rest of
the conversation. She already felt a bit
guilty for listening. 'Come on, Storm,'
she whispered, tiptoeing away.

Storm trotted at her heel as she
went into the kitchen. Beth felt her
anger drain away again, just like
when they were in the field earlier.
However annoying her cousin was,

she wouldn't wish that on anyone.

'Martin was actually telling the truth this time. He really did want to talk to his dad about something important. Ella must be very sick if Uncle Ollie thinks the vet should put her to sleep. Poor old girl,' she said to Storm.

Storm nodded, his midnight-blue eyes sad.

Ella was curled up in her basket in
the warm alcove. As Beth bent down to
stroke her, the old dog's tail thumped
against the floor.

Beth felt tears pricking her eyes.
'It's a shame that Ella's in such pain.
If she wasn't, she'd be able to enjoy
a few more months with Martin.'

Storm pricked his ears. 'I might be
able to help!'

Beth blinked at him. 'Really?
Can you use your magic to make
her young again?' she asked
hopefully.

'I am sorry, Beth. No magic can do
that,' Storm woofed gently. He padded
over and stood in front of Ella.

Once again, Beth felt the warm
tingling sensation down her spine.

Big gold sparks ignited in Storm's
fluffy black-and-white fur and the tips
of his ears sparked with magical power.
She watched as he huffed out a warm
glittery breath.

A shimmering golden mist
surrounded the old collie. For a few
seconds, pinpricks of gold danced all
around her like miniature fireflies and

then they sank into Ella's dull fur and disappeared.

Beth waited expectantly, but nothing happened. Ella looked just the same, with her grey muzzle and faded eyes.

Storm's magic didn't seem to have worked.

'Never mind. You tried. I guess magic can't be expected to do everything,' Beth said to Storm, trying hard to hide her disappointment as the last golden spark faded from Ella's fur. 'Let's go into the sitting room and find Martin. He's probably feeling really down. Maybe we can cheer him up.'

Storm had a gleam in his eye, but he just nodded. 'You have a very kind heart, Beth.'

'Anyone would do the same,' Beth

said, blushing. She always got embarrassed when people paid her compliments.

Martin was lying glumly on the sofa. Behind it, Beth could see the cabinet displaying the cups and trophies her uncle had won in ploughing competitions.

Oliver Badby sat at the table, working at the computer. He looked up and smiled as Beth and Storm came in. 'Hello. What have you two been up to?'

'We . . . I've finished cleaning up all the milk in the dairy. I thought Martin might like to go out with us or something,' Beth said.

Her uncle frowned and glanced at Martin. 'What's that about milk?'

'Er . . . nothing!' Martin said

hurriedly, getting up in a rush and hustling Beth out. 'Come on, Beth. Let's go and see if Mum needs any help with her shopping.'

'But she's not even back yet . . .' Beth protested, shaking off his arm.

'Duh! I know that! But Dad doesn't, does he?' Martin scoffed. 'And why did you have to mention the milk?'

But once in the hall, his shoulders slumped. 'Dad's been talking about taking Ella to the vet, to . . . to –'

'I know. I heard you talking to him,' Beth interrupted, feeling a lump rise in her throat. 'I'm so sorry.'

Martin shuffled his feet. 'Yeah, well. I know Ella's old and everything and I'm not ready to let her go, but Dad could be . . .' He lifted his head and looked

past Beth into the kitchen. She saw an
expression of complete amazement
come over his face. 'I don't believe it!'

'What?' Beth whipped round and saw
Ella padding out of the kitchen. The
old dog was moving easily. Her coat
looked glossy and her eyes were bright
and alert.

Ella trotted up to Martin and jumped
up to be stroked. 'Groof!' she barked

happily, wagging her tail and giving him a wide doggy grin.

'Look at her! It's like a miracle. She's not even limping!' Martin threw his arms round Ella and hugged her, burying his face in her fur.

Ella whined, licking him all over his face.

'Just wait until Dad sees her! There's no way he'll be taking her to the vet now!' Martin's face was lit up like a Halloween pumpkin.

Beth beamed with joy as she watched the two of them. She bent down to stroke Storm. 'Thanks again, Storm. This time from Martin and Ella. They're going to have a brilliant summer together,' she whispered.

Storm wagged his little tail happily.

Chapter
FIVE

'Ella seems to have found a new
lease of life since that pup arrived,'
Emily Badby said as she was clearing
away the lunch things the following
day.

Beth was helping her aunt stack the
dishwasher. She smiled, wishing that
everyone knew just how true that was!
But, of course, she would never tell

them or anyone else how magical Storm was.

Oliver Badby was finishing a cup of tea and Martin had just come back into the kitchen after taking some food scraps outside to the pig bin.

Storm was stretched out under the table. Suddenly his eyes flashed with mischief. Leaping out, he tore round and round the huge farmhouse table, his ears laid back and his tail streaming behind him.

Across the room in her bed, Ella's ears pricked up. With a spring in her step, she shot towards the cheeky pup and started chasing him. Storm suddenly swerved, leapt into her empty bed and plonked himself down. Ella jumped straight in after him. Seconds later, the

two of them were curled up together, licking each other.

Everyone laughed.

'That's one way to sneak into a warm bed! You know, Ella and Storm could almost be a mother and her puppy,' Martin said fondly.

Then they heard the rumbling sound of a heavy lorry drawing up outside in the yard. Martin ran to the window and looked out.

'It's here, Dad! The Fergy's arrived!' he shouted, dashing outside.

Beth's uncle and aunt went outside to look. Beth followed curiously, wondering what was going on.

A large flatbed truck stood in the yard. On the back of it, there was a tomato-red tractor. Oliver went to speak to the lorry driver and then they began the unloading. A few minutes later, the red tractor stood in the yard.

Martin walked round it, his eyes shining. 'It's mega-ace, isn't it?'

'I s'pose it's OK,' Beth said, shrugging. She couldn't see what was so exciting about a boring old bit of farm machinery.

'OK?' Martin gave her an incredulous look. 'Are you kidding? That's a 1952 Massey Ferguson tractor.'

Beth wasn't impressed. 'It's a bit old, isn't it? Does it still work?'

Her uncle chuckled. 'Fergy's going to work very well. Wait until you see her pulling a plough. She's going to help me win the cup in the vintage class at the ploughing competition in a few weeks' time.'

'Dad's county champion at ploughing,' Martin said proudly.

To Beth, winning things for making straight lines down a field seemed like a very weird thing to do. *Don't they watch much TV around here?* she thought.

Martin saw the scornful look on her

face. He flushed. 'There's a lot of skill
involved in ploughing, you know.
Dad lets me have a go sometimes and
I'm getting really good at it,' he
boasted. 'I'm going to get a licence
when I'm fourteen. Then I can
compete too!'

'You're doing all right, but you'll
need a lot more practice first,' his dad
said.

'I know that,' Martin said in a sulky voice.

Oliver patted his son on the shoulder. 'Fergy could do with a wash and brush up. She's pretty dusty after her journey. Any volunteers?'

Martin's head came up. 'Beth and I will do it. Won't we, Beth?'

Beth frowned. Cleaning a tractor was definitely not top of her 'fun to do' list. It was right at the bottom, next to cleaning smelly trainers. But Martin seemed in an unusually good mood, so she nodded.

'OK. I don't mind.' *But if he starts bossing me about again, I'm leaving him to it*, she thought.

Beth helped Martin collect buckets, sponges and cleaning liquid. Storm came outside and lay down with his chin resting on his paws as she and Martin started work.

'There's all kinds of ploughing, you know. Tractor-trailed, mounted, reversible. You have to be very skilled to work a plot and make tidy ins and outs,' Martin explained enthusiastically as he sponged soapy water over Fergy's bright-red bonnet. 'They have world championship competitions. One day Dad might be good enough to take part.'

Beth didn't reply. She was scrubbing hard at a greasy mark on Fergy's red mudguard.

'Hey! Are you listening? Or are you ignoring me deliberately?' Martin flicked soapy water at her.

'Who said that?' Beth joked and flicked water back at him.

Martin's eyes gleamed mischievously. 'Oh yeah!'

Beth dodged out of the way as another sponge full of water sloshed towards her. 'Missed!' she crowed.

Laughing, they flicked soapy water back and forth.

Beth giggled as she pushed her damp hair out of her eyes and crouched behind the tractor. She was smaller than Martin and managed to avoid getting too wet, but most of her soapy flicks found their mark.

Martin's T-shirt was soon drenched. 'Right! Now you're for it!' He grabbed the whole bucket and lifted it into the air.

'Don't you dare!' Beth shrieked breathlessly.

As she went to flick more water at Martin, a tiny shower of golden sparks crackled around her hand and tingled against her fingers. The soapy sponge shot out of her hand. It zoomed through the air with perfect aim and splatted in Martin's face.

'Phoof!' Martin spluttered. He took a step backwards and slipped over on to his backside, tipping the entire bucket of water all over himself.

Beth cracked up laughing. She was helpless. She glanced across at Storm who wore a wide doggy grin and wagged her finger at him, scolding him gently.

'Sorry, Beth. I thought he was going to hurt you!' Storm yapped.

Scowling, Martin slowly got up. His dark hair was plastered to his head and water was dripping off the end of his nose.

At the look on his face Beth tried to stop laughing, but her mouth kept

twitching. 'You should see yourself,' she gasped, holding her ribs.

Suddenly Martin burst out laughing too. 'That was a great shot – for a girl! Come on, let's get some clean water.'

Beth went with him to fill her bucket from the outside tap. Staying at Tail End Farm was starting to feel a lot better these days.

She was amazed at Martin. This was

the most friendly he'd been since she arrived. And all because they'd had a water fight and she'd beaten him. *I'll never understand boys*, she thought, as they finished cleaning the tractor.

Chapter
SIX

Beth stood in the barn beside her aunt and watched her milking the goats. Storm was sprawled on a pile of clean straw beside the pens.

Beth sighed. It had rained almost every day since she'd been here. Heavy rain was drumming on the roof once again. 'I'm getting fed up with this rotten weather,' she complained.

Emily smiled. 'You learn to take it in
your stride when you work on a farm.
But the goats really hate the cold and
the wet. That's why I brought them
into the barn, but I'd hoped they could
go out in their field again by now.' She
looked at her niece's glum face. 'Do
you want to have a go at milking?'

'I don't know,' Beth said doubtfully.

'Come on. Don't be shy. Stand here.

It's not very difficult and Daisy's a good milker,' Emily encouraged. She showed Beth how to take a firm but gentle hold and squeeze down with one finger at a time.

Beth took a deep breath and rested one shoulder against Daisy's flank. She followed instructions, a bit awkwardly at first. To her surprise, the milk began to flow into the bucket.

'Hey! I'm doing it!' she cried delightedly.

In a few minutes Beth felt like an expert. She filled a bucket and then strained the milk into the metal churn, feeling really pleased with her success. 'That was great. Maybe I'll ask Mum and Dad if we can have some goats. It would save Dad moaning about having to dig up all the weeds and we'd have loads of milk to give to all our friends.'

'Hmm. Remember that you'd have to milk them twice daily, summer and winter, seven days a week, in all weathers, just like I do,' her aunt cautioned, smiling.

Beth raised her eyebrows. 'On second thoughts, I think I'll stick to milk in cartons and leave the weeds to Dad!'

Her aunt laughed.

A loud triumphant braying came from the back of the barn. There was a stamping and clattering, followed by a rustling noise.

'Darcy?! What's he doing?' Beth said.

'It sounds like he's jumped out of his pen – again,' her aunt sighed. 'That goat's a proper menace. He's been cooped up for too long because of all this rain and he's got energy to spare. I'm going to have a real game trying to catch him.'

'Shall I help you?' Beth offered.

'You could go and see where Darcy's got to, if you like, while I close the barn door so he can't escape,' her aunt said.

'I will find Darcy!' Storm barked, darting to the back of the barn.

Beth hurried after him. As she reached the big stack of straw bales near the goat's pen, she spotted Darcy standing right on the very top of them.

'Look at him! He thinks he's the king of the castle!' Beth said.

Looking down his haughty nose, Darcy snickered as if he agreed. He

looked very pleased with himself for
having climbed up so high.

Storm wagged his tail and then
jumped up on to his back legs and put
his front paws on the bottom bale.
'Gr-oof!' his bright eyes flashed playfully.

'Watch out, Storm. That stack looks a
bit wobbly –' Beth began warily, but
before she could finish her sentence,
Darcy flexed his powerful back legs and
did an almighty leap in the air, right
over Beth and Storm's heads – and then
everything seemed to happen all at once.

The top straw bale wobbled wildly
from the force of Darcy's take-off and
slowly began to tip forward.

Beth's eyes widened in horror. Storm
had turned his head to watch Darcy
land on the barn floor a few metres

away and hadn't noticed the danger. The
bale was about to fall and land on him!

Without a second thought, Beth
threw herself forward. Her fingers just
touched Storm's fluffy black-and-white
fur and she managed to grab him.

Holding him close to her chest Beth rolled out of the way just in time. The heavy bale crashed to the ground and she felt the rush of dusty air as it missed them both by a fraction of a centimetre.

Beth let out a shaky sigh of relief. Still holding Storm, she pushed herself slowly to her feet. 'Are you all right?' she asked the shocked little puppy.

'Yes. You saved me, Beth. Thank you,' Storm woofed, reaching up to lick her chin.

'I couldn't bear anything to happen to you,' Beth said as she stroked Storm's soft ears. She felt a surge of affection for her tiny friend.

Glancing down the barn, Beth saw that her aunt had managed to get a rope on a subdued-looking Darcy and was leading him back to his pen. She frowned when she reached Beth and Storm and saw the straw bale on the floor nearby. 'I thought I heard something fall, but I couldn't be sure with all the noise Darcy was making. Are you OK? It's lucky you weren't badly hurt,' she said.

'Oh, it missed us by miles,' Beth said

lightly, not wanting to worry her aunt.

'Thank goodness for that!' Emily said, relieved. 'I'm responsible for you while you're here and your mum and dad wouldn't be very pleased with me if you had an accident. I'll get Oliver to come and see to that stack. Just let me tether this naughty goat in his pen first. He's full of surprises.'

Beth bit back a grin. *He's not the only one!* she thought.

'I'm sorry, Martin, I haven't got time to go out with you today. Maybe tomorrow. I'm planning to clear the unused bit of the top field and use that for practising ploughing, but I can't promise when I'll get round to it,' Oliver was saying.

'Aw, Da–ad. You've already been out on Fergy a couple of times. When am I going to get the chance to have a drive?'

Beth sat in the window seat in the sitting room with Storm curled on a cushion beside her. Her uncle and cousin were in the yard outside. Their voices floated in through the open window. 'Martin's obsessed with that dumb old red tractor, even though Uncle Ollie's told him it's too big for him to drive by himself.'

Storm's ears twitched and he gave a sleepy nod, tired out from all the excitement in the barn earlier.

Two minutes later, Martin burst into the room and plonked himself down next to Beth.

'Watch it! You almost sat on Storm!'
Beth complained.

'Sorry, Storm.' Martin stroked Storm's
fluffy black-and-white fur absently. 'Dad's
being a right pain! He won't let me near
Fergy unless he's with me. I know I can
handle driving her by myself, but he
won't believe me,' he grumbled.

Beth wisely chose to stay silent on
the matter. 'It's stopped raining at last.
Why don't we walk into the village
with Storm and Ella?' she suggested,
trying to cheer him up.

Martin's lip curled. 'Go shopping? I'd
rather watch paint dry. I'm going to
take Ella for a long walk over the fields.
By myself,' he said pointedly.

Beth got the message. She didn't
bother to tell him that she'd been about

to suggest that they went to the new
sports centre. 'Suit yourself.' She
shrugged, got up and called to Storm to
follow her.

'Where are you going?' Martin asked,
frowning.

Beth turned to him and tapped the
side of her nose with one finger in
what she knew was an annoying way.

Martin threw up his hands, got up and stormed out, muttering about 'stupid annoying girls' under his breath.

'Oh well. Martin's back to his usual self. His good mood didn't last long, did it?' Beth said to Storm. 'But I'm getting used to him now and I don't mind it so much. I think he just likes moaning!'

Storm nodded, blinking up at her with bright midnight-blue eyes.

Beth changed her mind about the sports centre. 'We'll go to the village by ourselves. I bet they have a pet shop that sells dog treats,' she decided.

Storm yapped excitedly, almost falling over his own paws as he bounded out of the door.

Chapter
SEVEN

Emily Badby had been baking bread all morning and the whole farmhouse smelled wonderful.

Beth sat in the cosy kitchen, reading a new computer magazine she'd bought at the village shop. Storm was curled up beneath the table, chomping on a bone-shaped dog chew and Beth could feel the tiny puppy's warmth against her feet.

It had just been raining again, but a watery sun was now beginning to push through the clouds.

Suddenly the faint sound of barking and growling interrupted Beth's peaceful morning. She tensed, listening hard. It seemed to be coming from far away, but then the noise stopped and Beth thought she must have been mistaken. Her aunt didn't seem to have noticed anything.

'Where's Martin?' Beth asked.

'Up at the top field. His dad's making a start on clearing it with Fergy and the old plough. Ella's with him,' Emily replied.

Making sure her aunt wasn't looking, Beth leaned over to whisper to Storm. 'I'll take you for a walk up there later.

It's no good waiting for Martin and
Ella to come back here. Wild horses
wouldn't drag him away if Uncle Ollie's
ploughing.'

There was no reply.

Frowning, Beth bent right over and
looked under the table. Storm had gone,
leaving the half-eaten dog chew lying
there.

That was odd. He'd never run off

without telling her where he was going before. She got up and went to look for him.

Storm wasn't in the sitting room or any of the other downstairs rooms. She went up to her bedroom, expecting to find him curled up on her duvet, but he wasn't there either.

'Storm?' she said, beginning to feel concerned.

A faint sound came from beneath her pillows. Beth smiled and swept back the top of the duvet to reveal a little black-and-white tail. 'What's this, hide-and-seek —' she began, but stopped at the sight of Storm trembling all over. 'What's wrong? Are you sick?' she asked worriedly.

Storm squirmed more deeply into the

pillows. 'I sense that Shadow knows where I am. He will send his magic, so that any dogs that are nearby will attack me,' he said in a muffled little whine.

'Oh no! That must have been what I heard. We need to find you a better hiding place. Maybe the barn or . . . or . . .' Beth racked her brains trying to think of somewhere safe.

'It is no use, Beth,' Storm whimpered, his deep-blue eyes as dull as stones. 'Leave me here for a while, please. Any dogs looking for me may pass by.'

'All right. If that's best,' Beth said. She had a sudden thought. 'What about Ella? Will Shadow's magic work on her too?' She felt horrified that the gentle old collie might become Storm's enemy.

'No. I have already used my magic to

help her. That will protect Ella from Shadow's evil,' Storm whined before he burrowed right under the pillows and curled up into a tight little ball.

Beth gently gathered his tail in, replaced the duvet and tucked it tightly round him. No one would know there was anything under the pillow. She went out quietly, hoping like mad that Storm's plan would work. She couldn't

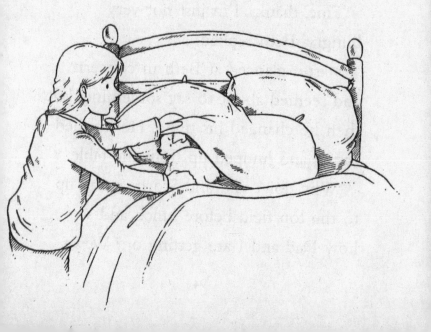

bear to think of her friend having to leave suddenly with no warning.

Beth could hardly eat any lunch for worrying about Storm. She nibbled a few mouthfuls of the delicious tomato salad and cauliflower cheese and then asked if she could leave the table.

'Are you feeling all right?' her aunt asked.

'Fine, thanks. I'm just not very hungry,' Beth replied.

Martin glanced at Beth in concern and seemed about to say something, but then he changed his mind. He finished eating and jumped up from the table.

'Why don't you and Storm come up to the top field before lunch and see how Dad and I are getting on? We've

cleared quite a lot of it already. I'm
going up there again now with Ella.
You could come with us, if you like.'

'I might do. I'll . . . um . . . follow
you up there in a minute,' Beth
murmured absently.

'Please yourself,' Martin muttered.

When he and Ella had left, Beth went
into the hall with a heavy heart. She
was dreading going upstairs to her
bedroom. Would Storm still be here or
had her friend already gone forever?

Suddenly, a tiny fluffy black-and-
white figure came bounding down the
stairs. 'Hello, Beth,' Storm barked
happily.

'Storm! You're still here!' Beth cried,
overjoyed, throwing her arms round
him.

Storm yapped and licked her face, his tail whirling madly. His midnight-blue eyes were as bright as a moonlit sky and he seemed completely back to his usual self. 'I cannot sense any strange dogs nearby, so they must have gone past. But if they return I may have to leave at once. We might not have time to say goodbye.'

'I understand,' Beth said, hardly taking this in. She just wanted to enjoy every single moment of the time they could now spend together.

She secretly hoped that Storm would stay with her forever, even though she knew he must someday return to help his injured mother and lead the Moon-claw wolf pack.

Beth decided to talk about something

else. 'Do you fancy going to watch Uncle Ollie giving Martin some ploughing practice? It'll probably be dead boring,' she said, pulling a face.

Storm's cute face lit up, as it always did at any chance of a walk.

Where's Uncle Ollie? Beth wondered as they walked towards the top field. She could see the red tractor and the plough mounted behind it, but only Martin and Ella stood beside it.

Storm was trotting beside her with his nose snuffling round on the ground.

Martin waved. 'Hi! I didn't think you'd bother coming,' he shouted, sounding surprised and pleased.

Ella spotted Storm. She wagged her tail and trotted over, barking a greeting.

'I thought we might as well. Storm loves playing with Ella,' Beth said, smiling at the dogs.

'Great. Now you can see what ploughing's all about. Watch this,' Martin called out. Leaping into Fergy's seat he started the engine and moved forward.

'Martin, don't! You're not supposed to be doing that!' Beth said worriedly, remembering her uncle's strict rules about Martin only driving under his supervision.

'I know what I'm doing!' Martin said

huffily. 'Anyway, I'll only plough a couple of furrows. Dad's just popped down to the barn for a can of lubricating oil – he'll never know. Unless you decide to tell him,' he said, looking hard at her.

'Thanks a lot. You should know by now that I don't snitch!' Beth said indignantly.

Martin looked uncomfortable and then he gave a wry grin and nodded. Concentrating hard, he held the large steering wheel steady, as the red tractor trundled slowly along, pulling the plough behind it. As he moved forward, the weedy turf was turned over and the soil curved away from the plough's metal mouldboards in rich brown waves.

Despite herself, Beth was fascinated by watching the furrows form. Martin leaned over to watch the back wheels, making sure he kept driving in a perfectly straight line. The new brown furrow folded itself over and was laid neatly next to one previously made.

Beth realized that ploughing took a lot of skill. 'You're pretty good at this, aren't you?' she said, impressed.

Martin threw her a smile over his shoulder, obviously enjoying himself and pleased by her praise. 'I'm not bad. But then I was taught by an expert. My dad!'

Suddenly Storm's head came up and his midnight-blue eyes flashed. Barking shrilly, he raced forward and began dodging back and forth in front of

Fergy's front wheels. 'Stop! Stop!' he
barked urgently.

'Martin! Watch out for Storm!' Beth
cried.

'Why's he doing that? Call him off!'
Martin shouted.

Beth frowned. It wasn't like Storm to
do something so dangerous without a
good reason. But she was too worried
about him getting hurt to try and work
out what that was.

'Come here, Storm! You'll get hurt!'
she shouted.

But Storm seemed beside himself.
Barking frantically, he ran even closer
to the tractor's ridged tyres, snapping at
them and growling. One of the wheels
passed by him closely, missing him by a
fraction.

As a stone flew out and hit him, Storm gave a loud yelp.

'Martin! Look out!' Beth screamed, sure that Storm was about to be run over.

Panicking, Martin swung the tractor's steering wheel to avoid the tiny puppy. Fergy slewed to a halt. Martin turned off the engine and jumped down.

'Look at that furrow. It's all wonky now. That stupid puppy's made me mess up!' he fumed.

Storm stood by, panting heavily, his little sides heaving.

'Hang on! What's that? Look!' Beth interrupted, pointing at something half buried in a weedy grass ditch that Martin had been just about to plough up. It was a brownish metal tube with a blunt end. As Beth leaned over for a closer look, her heart missed a beat. 'I think it might be a bomb!'

Chapter
EIGHT

'Don't be daft!' Martin said to Beth, striding over to have a look, but the moment he saw the metal object he frowned. 'Oh! You're right. It does look like a bomb. But it's probably been there for donkey's years. Look, it's all rusty and dented. I bet it's harmless.'

'Storm didn't seem to think so,' Beth reminded him.

Martin hesitated, chewing at his lip.

Beth guessed that he was worried about getting into trouble for driving the tractor. 'Martin, this is an emergency. We have to go and tell Uncle Ollie – now!' she said.

'You're right,' Martin decided. 'Come on!'

Beth didn't need telling twice. She bent down to pick up Storm and then

turned on her heel and ran. Martin and
Ella leapt after her and they all hurried
back towards the farm as fast as they
could.

Luckily Oliver was just coming
out of the barn with an oil can. He
raised his eyebrows when they raced
straight up to him. 'Where's the fire?'
he joked, but his face grew serious as
Martin and Beth began explaining.

'Well done, you two. You did the
right thing. Unexploded bombs
need expert handling. Right. I'll
phone the emergency services and
then alert the neighbours.' He took
his mobile phone out of his jacket
pocket and dialled. 'Martin, will you go
into the house and tell your mum,
please?'

Martin nodded, his face now pale with worry.

Beth realized that her cousin had only just begun to grasp how serious this really was. Now that they were all a safe distance from the bomb, she found herself shaking as it all sank in.

'Thank goodness you sensed the bomb was there. You were very brave to get so close to the tractor and risk getting hurt,' she whispered to Storm.

'I had to stop Martin somehow. We were too close for me to use my magic. Martin would have seen, but I could not risk anyone getting hurt,' Storm woofed gently.

Beth and Storm stood in the yard with Martin, Ella and her aunt as noisy police cars and fire engines arrived.

Farm workers and their families began gathering too.

Beth looked towards the top field, where blue lights from half a dozen police cars were now flashing. She could see at least four fire engines. Bright-yellow hazard tape had been strung all round the site of the bomb and across the field entrance.

'If it hadn't been for Storm making a pest of himself, I'd have ploughed straight over that bomb,' Martin said. He bent down to pat Storm's head. 'Thanks, boy. You might just have saved my life.'

'You are welcome, Martin,' Storm barked, wagging his tail, but of course only Beth could hear him speaking.

She beamed down at Storm, feeling

very proud of her brave little friend.

Oliver came up and put a hand on his son's shoulder. 'I should ground you for a week for driving Fergy when I particularly told you not to!' he said sternly.

'It wasn't my fault. Beth . . .' Martin started to make another excuse to get himself out of trouble, but then he seemed to think better of it and hung his head. 'Beth told me I shouldn't be driving Fergy by myself and she was right. I'm sorry, Dad.'

'You always are,' Oliver sighed. 'But on this occasion it was lucky for all of us that things have turned out this way. If I'd have been ploughing and not you, I probably wouldn't have seen the bomb until it was too late.'

Martin looked subdued as he took this in and realized what it could have meant. He was silent for a moment, and then he brightened. 'So I'm not in all that much trouble after all. Cool!'

'I give up!' His dad shook his head slowly and rolled his eyes.

'Look, someone in the field's waving a red flag,' Beth noticed.

Just then Oliver's mobile phone rang. He answered it and then spoke in a loud voice. 'Listen up, everyone. There's going to be a controlled explosion in a few minutes. We needn't be alarmed. We're quite safe here.'

Whump! A loud bang split the air.

Despite the early warning, Beth almost jumped out of her skin as the explosion echoed in her ears. An enormous spray of dark soil shot out in all directions and a thick dark plume of smoke drifted upwards.

'Yay! Way to go!' Martin shouted.

Everyone clapped and cheered. The danger was over.

'There'll be no more ploughing in

that field until the bomb squad have declared it safe. Do you hear me, Martin?' Oliver said.

'I wouldn't go up there now if you paid me,' Martin said.

Beth could see that he meant it this time. Martin really seemed to be changing and Beth realized that she'd actually grown quite fond of her grumpy cousin during her time at Tail End Farm!

'If you'd all like to come into the house I'll make coffee and there's freshly made cake,' Emily called out to everyone.

People began filing into the farmhouse. Martin called Ella to heel and followed them in. Beth was about to go in too, when Storm suddenly

whined with terror and streaked
towards the barn.

Beth heard a fierce growl behind her
and looked round. She spotted two
mongrel dogs running into the
farmyard. As Beth saw their extra-long
teeth and pale wolf-like eyes, she felt a
clutch of fear.

The dogs were under Shadow's spell.
Storm's enemy had found him!

Without a second thought, Beth raced into the barn ahead of the dogs. Somehow she knew where Storm would be. Darcy's pen!

She reached the pen at the back of the barn in time to see the tiny black-and-white puppy running into it. As the dogs pursuing Storm ran into the barn, there was a snort of rage and Darcy leapt right over the top bar of the pen and landed on the barn floor.

Braying threateningly, the billy goat ran straight at the fierce dogs with his head lowered. *Bang! Thud!* He butted them in the side, buying Storm precious time.

Suddenly there was a blinding gold flash and bright golden sparks rained down all around Beth and crackled on

to the barn floor. Storm was no
longer a tiny black-and-white puppy
but instead stood before her as a
young silver-grey wolf with glowing
midnight-blue eyes. At his side
was a huge she-wolf with a gentle
face.

Beth knew this was the moment that
Storm had to leave.

Storm lifted his magnificent head and
looked at her with sad eyes. 'Be of
good heart, Beth. You have been a true
friend,' he growled in a deep velvety
voice. He raised a large silver paw in
farewell and then he and his mother
faded and were gone.

There was a terrifying howl of
rage behind Beth. The mongrels' teeth
and eyes instantly returned to normal

and the confused dogs ran out of the barn.

Beth stood alone in the barn. A deep sadness welled up in her. She couldn't believe that Storm had left so suddenly. She was glad he was safe, but she was going to miss him terribly.

'I'll never forget you, Storm,' she whispered, her throat closing with tears.

She knew that she'd always treasure the time she had shared with the tiny magic puppy.

She heard steps behind her and turned to see Darcy coming towards her. He leaned forward to nuzzle her arm. 'You were really brave. Storm would be so proud of you,' she said, stroking him before leading him back to his pen. 'The sun's coming out. I think I'll ask Aunt Em if you can go out in the field.'

Darcy snickered delightedly as if he understood.

'Talking to yourself again?' Martin joked from behind her. 'Are you coming into the farmhouse? I've saved you a piece of cake.'

As Beth turned to look at her cousin,

she grinned. *Trust Martin to have the last word*, she thought, knowing somehow that Storm was watching them, his midnight-blue eyes glowing with approval.

Win a Magic Puppy goody bag!

The evil wolf Shadow has ripped out part of Storm's
letter from his mother and hidden the words so that magic puppy
Storm can't find them.

Storm needs your help!

Four words have been hidden in secret bones in the first
four Magic Puppy books. Find the hidden words and put them
together to complete the message from Storm's mother.
Send it in to us and each month we will put every correct message
in a draw and pick out one lucky winner, who will receive
a Magic Puppy gift – definitely worth barking about!

Send the hidden message, your name and address on a postcard to:
Magic Puppy Competition
Puffin Books
80 Strand
London WC2R 0RL
Good luck!

puffin.co.uk

Coming Soon

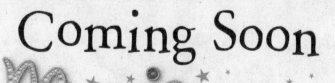

Magic Puppy

A little puppy,
a sprinkling of magic,
a forever friend.

SUE BENTLEY

Magic Puppy

A New Beginning
9780141323503

Muddy Paws
9780141323510

Cloud Capers
9780141323527

Star of the Show
9780141323534

puffin.co.uk